Drawing the Blue part o

1. ....
2. ....
3. ....gratitude from inside the edge of the world
4. ....what would Mary Magdalene do?
5. ....Ritual Magic
6. ....A pharaohs' breath
7. ....Earth School Damage
8. ....Of the Wolf
9. ....To my medicine friends
10. ....The Flying Dream
11. ....For Keshet
12. ....Flags off
13. ....Loon
14. ....What did the child soldier give to the light being?
15. ....//Widening
16. ....For Will, from B4 the storm
17. ....Off road
18. ....LA Lyft driver
19. ....Grabbing onto grace stains
20. ....Time Travelling
21. ....The gods we made up believed in us
22. ...."The metaphysics of the heart are ancient"
23. ....Back in that temple
24. ....Wild love crept in me
25. ....Being alive is strange (R U still awake)
26. ....If not you
27. ....I begin in a rude place
28. ....Saint Chiron
29. ....Ask the Wind
30. ....The heart of my ray beings
31. ....I can remember a medicine womyn
32. ....What I can't say
33. ....Decorate this womb space
34. ....Skyscraper Syndrome
35. ....Back Home
36. ....Brooklyn Fairy Style
37. ....The Noiselessness of Rainbow Cricket Music
38. ....To the heart of a stolen planet
39. ....A Childish Ghost
40. ....Awkward prayer
41. ....The Untouchable Malachite/Baby $kripper
42. ....$$PTSD$$
43. ....Backwash
44. ....Amber and earwax
45. ....I want the lake to go skinny dipping in me
46. ....Drawing the blue flame
47. ....Stay

48..To the body inside my body
49..All Net
50..As Above So Below

Sí tu, Muerte

You torched a city of 12 wombs because you thought that was your mother
"**Sí** tu, muerte"
I feel I have no power
Though I smuggle you through my chest like a diamond

Notes on blood disease

accepted passing in Florida swamps and said "yes, ok,"
and stopped being afraid
t's not a big deal, I can make my body infinite sized
There is no linear
One stop on the train, your lips turning blue as Hudson river death
and the next awake
n a luke warm bathtub inside the earth annoyed and laughing with me
I don't know how to speak any more
Next week I'll be rid of this grief infection in my left eye
the same like when Grandma Morgan died
or awake to a woman screaming at the park
He says, pointing at the gun,
"you can never ever shoot yourself with this... but this is America."
He says, "it really is poison so why are you laughing?"
I say, "cos I know"

gratitude from inside the edge of the world

((((do u keep a small poem
about the moon inside your storm
at all times
and if so
will u tell it to me)))))

Times I drew a foxhole with a sharpie
 And then colored in the Sky, it's a you- shaped
Hole/ gratitude from inside the edge of the world
there's a space between the fractures
And the holy humming
Face it dude, gods been skied up in the parking lot
It's not you, it's the colonial belt
Around the neck
I once put a mermaid baby
inside a man's belly
so he would have something to protect inside
the dark caves of his dreaming
And you
carry moonbeams in your stomach

<u>what would Mary Magdalene do?</u>

Wasn't the body always for sale?
That's not what the onions know
their roots and bulbs laid out like mermaids in the dirt
I've been looking for Mary Magdalene in the pockets of the men
who built these temples
meanwhile she's thunder and lightning in a ravens' throat
flooding the gown of the pavement

Ritual Magic

ritual magic is flooding the basement of my brain with sunlight
each time i bust my head thru the tv soundtrack
i bleed so strangely it scares the doctor
and what to do with so much meaninglessness
hung upside down in Indras' net
the radio kid sings, "all my friends are dead"
selfishly do i honestly believe
I've lost my power again
scribbling lopsided incantations
prescriptions from guardian angels who push hibiscus flowers thru my left eye
while i make scalar waves with my hands

A pharaohs' breath

ribs of a hollowed out dog
stained with ghost tears of Arizona
her voice, the moons' body, a pharaohs' breath
we were two shadows scaling the fence
held by the rivers' prayers
(and the nomadic tendencies of stars in a body)
even in the town where you stayed
entirely still
scent of your wingspan, a blue flame bouquet
of tattooed skin regrown by honey
i will always always miss your magic
even while the infinite grabs me and holds me by the infinite
will you call me by my name in a language-less song?
sweet thieves resting at the paws of the temple

Earth School Damage

the most painful thing
i think we are taught to hate ourselves
more than we love each other and how do we unlearn this
when Eli Coppola was dying she wrote
"instead of religion i studied the ocean" and
"i just want to meet someone else who is happy"

Of the Wolf

How do I explain myself?
You are a sky ship, blood
You are the weirdest angel
You are the sound that I'll take when I leave this earth
You are the x-ray of roots beneath the sidewalk
You are the heart of the wolf in a doves' throat

<u>To my medicine friends</u>

a nocturnal rainbow, an alphabet made of tiger tracks
cinnamon onyx currency
an orchestra of wing beats & bricks
you felt a heartbeat in the nest
rattlesnakes hustling their lonely rattle
Flags off your dreaming skins
Do you kiss like a warrior taking off their paint
Do you kiss like the soft skull of a baby gods' head
Do you kiss in the bluest part of the flame

The Flying Dream

Living weird
like a child god
learning to face my death
awkward like a feather
coming out a coyotes' neck
Green can I call you that
melted like blood in a
trip for a vein when you
say - can I peace out now
Lay low and meadow tho
Breathe in the meadow slow
Sun puddle strut your mouth
Kiss with a parking lot
Heavy how hit or not
Guess is what I can find
Digging into that ground
Light like a god on you
Dreaming how dreamers do

<u>For Keshet</u>

Trembling held
so finally held
see thru
Malachite
Kiss and fly weather of your soul
Kite on my bones
Bloody massacre// Blood line massacre
Soaks thru our hair and napkins
the devil would never play poker for your heart
Leave that shit to white Jesus
Sit back down, nothing is your fault today.
Again. Somebody goes,
A breakdancing unicorn messiah
Up a mountain
I am healing I am healing
I am healed

Flags off

I was born with the stolen stones in my mouth
I was born swallowing some
and spitting some out

Loon

what can't you hear
past the bough
of hearts exploding for you
I'm early
morning clean
softer than a mockingbird
softer than wading
thru another woman's bones

What did the child soldier give to the light being?

What did the child soldier give to the light being?
What kind of secret handshake also doesn't bend time
say my heart is astrally projecting in refraction
"I keep you at arms' length for a reason"
like a snake in the basement licking Cassandras' feet
a song from my future
where we speak in tree talk
or all the things the doctor couldn't pronounce in my language
like what to call the spiderwebs in my legs
I'd tell you about Bronx angels hanging out on laundry lines
but I'm not a poet..

Widening

taking the dust off my hips:
clocks, heads, full moon officers.
I was looking for you because I know your audience
An unopened chest full of meteorites and grass, mine too
I forgot to mention how when I was a kid
I took baths with the werewolf families' kids
on the full moon and on holidays.
You give me lightning rocks & ghost pennies
You give me small words covered in lace
& fire engines that vibrate at the frequency of hummingbirds
I slept till we reached the desert
I come from the middle of the earth or not at all
I just want to make a fire in your garden

For Will, from B4 the storm

if this flood kisses me
I'll wash my lungs
if my heart sheds like water
I'll cross the street
satellite orbiting sleep backwards
in my chest
100 wolves scattering
the highways' throat for a drum.
Fingerprints as a posture for a postage stamp
I'm listening
Easier than 3 bullets in his brain
the font of your music on my bones replanting a nervous system
sleep, sleep
the milky ways' ghost graffiti-ing sleep
Will, Bronx-bound, journeying, the dreamers' syndrome always following us
as junk piled up
healing a mermaids' torn pussy, I mean
blankets
Do earthquakes practice being themselves?
Earthquakes don't practice being.
Earthquakes don't practice being.
I am also Saturn for blood and artemisinin
I regret not giving myself as a gift to the rain in awkward currents
sharpening my sounds like knives
swimming around inside a rainbow octave
a little lust pocket
I keep this light in my back pocket as a crows' foot which is fuckin stupid.
(but) If your blood is also a funny shape then yell
If your blood is also a funny shape then yell
It's not like the moon can't hear you

Off road

see i just hadn't heard
that voice in awhile
arguing for my spirit
i think we were drawing
a map of Rainwater
in a country with no location

LA Lyft driver

Ex monk bad boy tattooed sacred skull
ninja turtle jasmine rosary
He said a smile is Gods' jewelry
I told him about the light body
he said animals always know
He said his master was a bad boy too
Who chanted and tattooed his back and head
he said, it's a secret but I'll show you
You gotta go see the elephants
Believe in the universe
watch tv, learn spanish, stay happy

<u>Grabbing onto grace stains</u>

I am drawing an escape route for my friends
All skied up
With Flames in them
I trip on books of bridges
Scars stacked up
With our mom's crow zippers
& grabbing onto grace stains
I give, you give me
Mouth to mouth
But how can I explain
Unconditional love
While I'm still sleeping
On top of your gills

Time Travelling

All i can remember is
dreams about
animals in the junkyard
u wear your freestyle like Charlie Browns' blanket
leaving crescents
sand in my shoes, moon stains
beautiful smells
peach pits spat out
Bronx bound
how we took a breath
Shed snake skin wears a body
ribs cracked open with relief song
your voice is a gun made of lace
spitting birds' nests out of church bones
My voice is a shy weather god
sleeping in the left ear of a Chernobyl wolf.

The gods we made up believed in us

She dreams
we dream
sea dreams
The un-hunted lioness heart
Swirling secret defibrillator
I am nothing but a black cat
Discount prices not effecting my poor wooden honor
Quiet bones licking each others' mattresses
Summoning a salad bowl
Like a shipwreck you're so happy to see
Through the sidewalk
by breathing
I am not a viking, but we clean our muscles this way
She dreams a ship shaped house
A rocking chair built from an x-ray of an orchestra
A man standing on the corner asking for a pack of lightning
In exchange for his secret bones
His lioness heart
I know I can know outer space through sleep
All this blessed and beautiful soil under my attack blood
Sun babies breaking bread
For the morning
For a drought in paper candles
For a lick of tiger ice cream

"The metaphysics of the heart are ancient"

Many times metaphysics caused me
to cross continents from the bottom of the ocean where its black
to the other side of my body
Will you lay in the wind
Can I sing in your womb?
doctors who are men who never ask
permission to touch my body
Large worlds and their trashed faces
Night body: Did you see that moon?
Pull that big yellow world down
and step inside of it
It can only be softest warm and safe
There is so much I want to love you with

Back in that temple

I took a vacation to Hades
to see the faceless roots womyn
and all I got was this lousy blanket
A constant conversation in constellations
Shook me from my body of shame
Made a night well out of everything
Back in the boxing ring
I wanted to move
but I had to lie down in the backwoods
by the exit sign (Hades)
Some million dollar ghosts chanting
pixelated thru the radio
I wanted to sing
but my heart was moving sideways
Blood, rust, gills,
I wanted to dance but
I was taught to cum like a scarecrow
Back In that temple
Hades rummaging thru womb space
dipping her fingers in the beautiful mud and Asphodel
calling the beast to turn the skies over
Please
Sing to me a little so I can be weightless
And so I can move for the first time
Again

Wild love crept in me

I have forgiven myself for attempting to buy back my halo
For believing that it was ever for sale
In the first place

Being alive is strange (R U still awake)

shipwrecks are the weirdest gods
you'd have to be a blues singer
like everyone else is
or share a shit mattress with an alligator
who's in charge of your dream obstacle course
one opal tooth in the back
so beautiful and dangerous
all the damage in your head finally makes sense
when you swallow it
I made small fires all over the country
made awkward love to a piano
and have only talked to desert ghosts recently
about the differences between wings
they tell me being alive is strange
and then your name in the snow
on the edges of me

If not you

Like cinderella smuggling gills
I am only 5 types of rain
& then nothing
I sleep underground
Is your body a forest fire
who is that witch tied to your ankles
is it you?
"If not you then who then"

<u>I begin in a rude place</u>

I begin in a rude place
praying awkwardly
my body is ugly and a consequence of silence
I watched myself being born
I came from crocodile mouths,
I swam thru the Bronx of my mothers' belly
she married those cracks in bible passages
her jesus-witch-brew cried a liquid city
between thighs and blurred bookcases
until a heartbeat broke centuries
a noisemaker spat
and bled thru his golden horn.
a poet held me down on a bed.
this is old news, all the stethoscopes have told it before.
I watch the singing ones
and I want to move in their throats
and I want to sleep in them
and wake
and not be so scared all the time.
I don't want to talk about the kissing ones
or the ones who are smaller than their mouths
who die in the middle of the street
and how small children are chastised for wanting to touch them.
Who are the lullaby gods' worst...
or the funk-smell that follows them across bridges
and beneath breasts
and powders armpits with their crying.
If I could tell you I love you
in a language where fear didn't exist
I know I would remember the earth as a piece of my chest.

Saint Chiron

I found out that I was Chirons' first cousin
I had been orbiting myself for a long time
The moon and her green moss gods
Angels flirt in numbers
Was it you trying to teach me
When I begged
to trade in your lessons
For wonder

Ask the wind

I'm rooted like the echoes of trees
Cloud hands littering the streets
Like a storm on a leash
Who walks infinity tightrope scared of a blind man listening in on a light beam (me)
I aim to swallow the sun and not burn
I put my ear to the chest of any living thing
And ask the wind why it hurts to write things down

"The heart of my ray beings"

Last night I fell through booby trap time
to a karaoke faucet where I was the music dripping into the cows' mouth
the skull of my past life ate hospital jello
to distract my inner children from their midnight bank robbery dreams.
Next, I adopted the demon child of myself
I held him to the "*heart of my ray beings*
who transcend felt walls"
"Did you bring the thunder wrapped in the right kind of blanket, space brother??"
"Yes, I'm hiding the soul of redemption
in my pajamas"

<u>I can remember a medicine womyn</u>

whose owl face I painted like a humyn
She bled blue on the bed
day after day
The arthritis from her numbed out guitar hands
we played in rainbow frequency
We hitchhiked the breeze
easy as stealing thunder from a temple

What I can't say

what I can't say in words
I try to cry thru the guitar
sloppy long necked bird
in my hands
why, when I cry
do I feel like I'm pick-pocketting my own chest

Decorate this womb space

I grew a wolf lung instead of a child
A head half smeared with sky
Wandered into my clogged-up rosaries
And moved in circular wings
This is my body, it won't be given up for you, but
How come you never leave an ear in a bowl of water by the door anymore?
I used to wash you with my poems

Skyscraper Syndrome

there was the sky
who wrestled me from the dirt
I awkwardly put on my human head
to love you with
I cut my teeth
into graffiti powder
to make a home
for homeless third eyes
and couldn't stop my body from howling

Back Home

in my dream i was on the deck of a hunting ship
Crawling into the empty body of a kid whale
so he wouldn't be scared while his spirit crossed over
Inside the walls of dark sticky skin
I traced a line of constellations
across the sky
for his spirit to follow home
Afterwards I could speak in whale language
And when I awoke Eero called me
Kid-whale spirit

Brooklyn Fairy Style

Sky splitting open/
the light magnets inside/
birds heads, their compasses for flight/
my compass towards you for flight/
my friends who are ghosts catcalling heaven,
my friends cat calling is heaven
I want to give you this small purple flower,
bench pressing clouds Brooklyn fairy style/
Venus moving backwards her geometry is covered in/
sacred and annoyed cows/
and kisses, all kinds of spit swaps
names for snow or storms or alchemy
and other earth school casual nighttime breakfast

The Noiselessness of Rainbow Cricket music

Get a haircut. Light yourself on fire. Eat a tree
Gasp up some nighttime into a toilet
Levitate. Ease your brakes
Pull oil with holy water at a carwash inside your mind
Cough less stars. Eat chicken with antibiotics
Pull a tiny line straight.
Move all infections to the wound inside the moon.
She says she won't take shit but turns the garbage into sleep
Kiss an imaginary goddess
Live with your forest, its beauty, it's toxicity
take all scabs off the sky from the sky scrapers
Laugh heady with scarecrows.
Tell them they don't have to laugh at what isn't funny
Choose which cartoon to be
Rotate in functional snowstorms
Keep your body a body.
What is old? The functionality of your wings.
Bless yourself with the noisiest rainbow
what are you afraid of?
I can't feel nothing
the noiselessness of rainbow cricket music
But I won't have time for that

To the heart of a stolen planet

I don't know what I keep in my sleeve
gentle rat
ghosts
lady painter ghosts,
freckled laughing fairy
ghosts.
I am holding the skeleton of a bird
gently
up against my stomach
don't be scared to speak
in extinct languages
the frequency of its missing wing
is the light
filling my chest
with slippery music
buttering the street into streams
clean enough
to sweat from that singing
and to be
baptized
in it

A childish ghost

I was a weird dream the desert had
Awkward pickpocket
Space suit too fragile for rain
An unusual purple flower
Was growing on her eyelids,
So she blinked.
I was a childish ghost
With a swollen face
& a big crooked moon tattoo
For a heart

<u>awkward prayer</u>

After Bob Kaufman

kerry says "holy ghosts of girlhood"
we stay playing strip poker
with the leaves changing
"billie holiday got lost on the A train and never came home"
I'm trying not to pass out
I'm a shot glass of infinite and nervous system decay
resting by the highway
2 young fawns grazing
deer portal while I take my meds
"I'm just a dumb humyn" I say
"I love you," I say
I bow my head in awkward prayer,
Lazarus touching gills with the dirt
in Venus tapestry
planets moving backwards
in sacred geometry
we stay dying and coming back

The Untouchable Malachite/ Baby $kripper

"talk dirty' he says
Baggy t-shirt clunks to the floor
'I'm not from here' I say proudly lifeless.
'I am the goddess of never not broken'
Easy hundred bucks in twenty minutes.
'Tell me about yourself'
My Jaguar mask crouches on my head like a hat
'I'm from Saturn...the streets have never been paved there.'

$$PTSD$$

I would sing you this song but it's a secret
I identify with Saturns' limbic system
at the bottom of the sea
I only want to talk about it with you
if you have that same scar in the same shape
Mary Magdalene's ghost coming from your torso
like a shipwreck
I open your mouth from afar
and pour blood soup from the center of the galaxy
gentle warriors
how strange and scary it is to be a body
in decay
I stuff my heart in a tree behind the gas station
a portal is shaped like a baby deer
we can talk shit like kali all day
for medicine

<u>Backwash</u>

I miss smoke
letters kissing the inside and glow
astronauts and their rituals
there's always a zombie apocalypse
in the basement of my brain
or a hungry tiger
everything is metal and water and air
a DJ playing where's god on repeat
back and forth
over an encyclopedia
barbecue of facts about animal hearts
somebodys' pockets are full of sugar
but I don't care.
I want to know If I can make it snow…

<u>Amber and earwax</u>

I buried my heart in the
twilight cow-field
Large feral horned
beasts
Make me feel safe
The way fire always has
Something as feral
As the biting wound in me
"An open window"
"you can drink
from my veins"
Stepping over and around rocks
Carefully
Wilderness says "if you see a rattlesnake
sing to it"

I want the lake to go skinny dipping in me

I want the lake to go skinny dipping in me
I want the lake to go skinny dipping in me
I want the lake to go skinny dipping in me

Drawing the blue flame

A year ago I awoke to a voice
from my dreaming yelling
"it's haram! It's haram!"
When I dragged my feet
from the astral realm
and tried not to come back from the dreaming….
In Arabic meaning "it's a sin, it's a sin"
and Tahani said it means that
it's a sin not to go back into your body
(or she would've left long ago)
Now I'm back to burning flags
ancestors suicide bombing nazis
ACAB for Noach and Palestine
and Harvey down in Burningham drawing the blue flame
in Martin Luther
as he turned his back to the open mouth of a gun as a dare
the long horn holding me in her horns cradling
the Brooklyn street in me from shoulder to hip check

stay

the reasons to stay
aren't always believable
Somebody left a pile of piano keys
beneath the underpass
We pressed palm to p(s)alm
Weeping from the whale belly
crawling the octaves of his voice
A constellation named after a hunter
scoops us back into her womb
2 snakes coiling in the empress of stillness
I call out to you in cellular poetry
the bars of language begging me to sit back down
the black box theatre of my chest
full of smuggled sky and doves
The old man beside me laughing under blankets
playing chess with death

I'm writing to the body inside my body

Who escapes
Who has had to end up
living
Driven wild
Like a hurricane that riots over my love letters
It's a curse, all the beautiful ways to describe a body decaying
So I stopped writing poetry
Focus on the weather channel
It's Like a tv show on doubt
So we can recognize
Every crude unicorn
Inside
Every make shift stable
My body is a wreck
stained graffiti shapes
I've never known how to take up space
Between what is stolen
And the soaked place where the sky belongs
Across the right side of my head
Between your thumb and forefinger
all I need is a stamp
a honeycomb
for homeless 3rd eyes
finding things shipwrecked
guts.
lusty moon syndrome

All Net

You were a lighthouse like Antigone
Coins pressed, one on each eyelid
Protection from the shock of your own bones
Like medusa burying a snake from her head
she wrapped him like an umbilical cord
A crooked altar in a kitchen playground cemetery
I was learning to bake cakes around suicide gods
nervous that I might sit inside their mouths for too long
I came to holding a carnival ticket to the womb
from the bottom of the sea
I dare you to love yourself
I found an angel to haunt me sweetly
A potbellied unicorn headed
old New York-Italian basketball coach
He would criticize my shots from the benches.

As Above So Below

I had a wounded vision of Asclepius w sparkling fake eyelashes
Coming out from under
The cosmic sewage battle
Conducting low frequency streams of light down your throat
To scare the demons
Who beat you up in the parking lot till u wished them infinite compassion and they fled
I walked up a tree today praying
my shadow gaping open like Peter Pan
Don't mind the infinite getting close
Visiting ghosts
Following a trail of wet paws thru hades

Printed in Great Britain
by Amazon